HEATED MATING

Savannah Stuart

Copyright © 2011, 2014 by Savannah Stuart

All rights reserved. Except as permitted under the U.S. Copyright Act of 1976, no part of this publication may be reproduced, distributed, or transmitted in any form or by any means, or stored in a database or retrieval system, without the prior written permission of the author. Thank you for buying an authorized version of this book and complying with copyright laws. You're supporting writers and encouraging creativity.

Cover art: Jaycee of Sweet 'N Spicy Designs
Author website: www.savannahstuartauthor.com

Publisher's Note: This is a work of fiction. Names, characters, places, and incidents are either the products of the author's imagination or used fictitiously, and any resemblance to actual persons, living or dead, or business establishments, organizations or locales is completely coincidental.

Heated Mating/KR Press, LLC -- 1st ed.

ISBN-10: 1942447132
ISBN-13: 9781942447139

eISBN: 9780996087490

Praise for the books of Savannah Stuart

"Fans of sexy paranormal romance should definitely treat themselves to this sexy & fun story." —Nina's Literary Escape

"I enjoyed this installment so much I'll be picking up book one...worth the price for the punch of plot and heat."
—Jessie, HEA USA Today blog

"...a scorching hot read." —The Jeep Diva

"This story was a fantastic summer read!" —Book Lovin' Mamas

"If you're looking for a hot, sweet read, be sure not to miss Tempting Alibi. It's one I know I'll revisit again and again."
—Happily Ever After Reviews

"You will not regret reading the previous story or this one. I would recommend it to anyone who loves a great shifter story."
—The Long & Short of It

"...a fun and sexy shapeshifter book and definitely worth the read."
—The Book Binge

PROLOGUE

Planet Lumineta, 2235

As Linc stared at Saroya's exposed back, he understood his dead brother's love of the dark-haired beauty.

The funeral pyre burned before them and the entire clan. The firelight played off the sheer shift Saroya wore. Compared to what most of the females of the clan wore her clothing was more than acceptable but he hated that the material dipped low, exposing most of her back. The arch of her spine was delicate and beautiful. He wanted to trace his fingers up the length then follow with his tongue. Unlike the females of his people, Saroya and the handful of other women they'd rescued from the dying blue planet were smaller, more fragile. Not weak, they'd proven that much. Just different in some ways.

Ever since his brother Gage had returned from that fateful mission with Saroya and ten other foreign females in tow, Linc had cursed the Goddess that he'd busted his knee up the week before and Gage had met her first.

If he hadn't hurt himself during training he'd have been on that mission. A mission his scholarly brother had only been on to collect data. And Linc would have seen Saroya first. She'd have been his and *only* his. It didn't matter that his society consisted mainly of male-female-male joinings. And it didn't matter that Gage and Saroya had tried to welcome him into their bed on more than one occasion. None of that shit mattered because he didn't share.

He would not share her. With anyone. Not even his own brother. So he'd always declined their invitations. He couldn't be sure but she seemed to think he preferred the opposite sex. That was fine with him. Let her have her assumptions.

A few wisps of her dark hair had come loose from the clip she'd secured it with. As he watched her, he noted a small tremble race through her. His people didn't show much emotion but hers were very different as he'd learned over the past six moon cycles. Though he couldn't see her face, he knew she was crying. Linc wanted to reach out and comfort her but he was a warrior. That wasn't done.

When she shifted her weight forward, as if she were ready to throw herself off the cliff and onto the burning pile of her lover's remains, he felt his entire fucking world shift. He nearly lost a century of his life.

Lightning fast, Linc lunged at her and wrapped his arm around her waist in a hard, tight grip. Even if she wanted to leave this life, this planet, he would not let her. Could not. He refused to live in a world where she didn't exist.

She struggled against him, silently crying until he twisted her around to face him. Barely reaching his chin, she wouldn't look at him as she beat his chest a couple times with her fists. Her words were incoherent and laced with grief. He was pretty sure she called him a heartless bastard too. He wasn't sure why, but the words pierced him. Hard. That was his brother slowly turning to ash down there. He was hurting too, even if he couldn't show it. And he hated himself for wanting his dead brother's mate so badly.

Just as suddenly, she stopped fighting and molded against him. Her arms wrapped around him and she buried her face against his neck. Shame burned through him as the rest of the clans present tried not to stare at the spectacle they made. No one but

Saroya and his brother knew that theirs had not been a true bonding. That only Gage and Saroya had been lovers. That he'd just been a roommate. Now surely everyone knew that she'd preferred his brother over him.

Goddess, he needed a drink. Her wet tears streamed down the back of his neck and onto his shoulder as her slender body pressed to him. To his absolute *fucking* horror he felt his cock growing. With her soft body molded against his it was impossible to control himself. He, a trained warrior of Lumineta, could not rule his body.

Thankfully she seemed oblivious because she just held him tighter. "Get me out of here." Her voice was shaky and thick with tears against his neck.

Without pause or apology, he turned and hurried toward one of the transport platforms. He would do anything she asked, even if it meant leaving his own brother's funeral. Gage would understand. Still holding her tight, he punched in the code to their home. Moments later they stood in their main living space. The once bright fire burning in the stone hearth had dwindled considerably.

As soon as she realized where they were, Saroya shook herself and stepped away from him. Her electric blue eyes glittered with unshed tears. They looked like the bright gems found deep in Lumineta's mountains. As rare as she was.

"I'm sorry." Her voice was soft, hoarse.

He frowned, and against his better judgment, he cupped her cheek. Touching her was like touching fire but at this moment he didn't care. He'd just lost his brother and the only female he'd ever cared about stood before him in pain. "For what?"

She ducked his gaze and stared at the stone floor. Her hands plucked at the sides of her shift. "For shaming you. I should have controlled myself."

He forced her chin upward with his finger. "You have nothing to be sorry for. I don't care what anyone thinks."

As their eyes locked, her blue ones filled with too many emotions for him to register. Confusion, pain and something he didn't understand. Finally she spoke but her voice was strained. "Will you be bringing someone else into our union after the mourning period?"

"No!" The word came out louder and sooner than he'd intended. He hadn't expected the question. Though maybe he should have. With the higher ratio of males to females, it was standard practice among his people to bring in another male after six moon cycles. But that wasn't going to happen. Even if his leader demanded it. He would not. Not for anyone.

Her brows knitted together. "Then you wish to let me choose . . . someone else?" Her voice cracked on the last word as more tears spilled down her cheeks.

Had she lost her mind? "Why would you ask that?"

Confusion and a trace of hurt clouded her expression. "You've never touched me. Barely look at me. I thought you might want me out of your house. Maybe I'm not your . . . preference?"

If he looked at her too much the pain made it difficult to breathe. "You were my brother's female and this is your house too."

Her frown deepened. "According to your culture, I'm yours too. We're technically mated. Unless you decide you don't want me."

He sighed. It had taken most of her females many moon cycles to get used to his people's way of life. Some still hadn't chosen males. Saroya had taken to their way of life quickly because of her feelings for his brother. The speed with which she'd embraced their world had made it even harder to keep his hands off her. But he hadn't been willing to touch her when it had been so obvious she loved his brother. It didn't matter that he'd been within his rights. Why would she want him, a scarred warrior? He struggled to find the words without confusing her. "I don't share."

She tucked her bottom lip between her teeth as she digested his words. "So you *do* wish for me in your bed?"

"No, *yes*. I..." Was there a right answer to her question?

Her eyes flared for a moment, then she shook her head. "I don't even know why I'm asking about this now," she muttered as if she were speaking to herself.

Before he could think of a response, she turned and strode from the room. The soft-soled slippers she wore were silent against the cold floor. Every fiber inside him told him to go after her, to comfort her, but his legs wouldn't listen.

CHAPTER ONE

Six Moon Cycles Later

"We need to do this more often. I mean . . . Oh, hell, I know you've been in your mourning period. I didn't mean it like that," Leilani muttered, her cheeks tinging pink as she looked at Saroya.

Smiling, Saroya shook her head. "I know what you meant, and you're right. I miss you and Brianna." Six moon cycles had passed since her mate's death and her mourning period was officially over. Not that she needed a damn clock to tell her when she could or could not be sad. She would always miss Gage, but after escaping a dying planet, she knew how fragile life could be. And Gage wouldn't have wanted her to mourn forever.

"That woman is so sweet, I can't believe I haven't spent more time with her." Leilani shook her head and took a sip of her dark red *villana*.

Saroya had chosen a lighter gold *villana* tonight, wanting something sweeter. "No kidding. You two are so similar." Not to mention they worked at the same architecture firm. But Saroya knew that they were in different departments and had different jobs altogether. Brianna was behind a lot of the designs and Leilani was a super assistant. That wasn't actually her job title but it was what Saroya thought of her as. She was so organized and put together.

"What's going on with you? I'm so glad you're finally getting out but . . . where's Linc? I thought he'd have stayed closer to the planet with, you know." Leilani's dark eyes filled with concern as she watched her.

Leilani was from a small group of islands from the dying planet they'd been saved from. Her dark hair was swept up into some complicated twist of loose braids on the back of her head and her bronze skin seemed to glow year round. To say she was beautiful would be an understatement. They'd already had four different males try to buy them drinks tonight and they'd only been at the restaurant for less than half an hour.

Saroya cleared her throat and looked down at her tulip-shaped glass. "Work is good for him, I think." Because she didn't actually know. Linc had up and left almost directly after Gage's death. The stupid part of her had thought that they might actually get to know one another, maybe even become friends if not lovers. But, he was gone and barely contacted her at all.

Leilani snorted. "What about you? I thought . . . I guess I just don't understand the culture yet. I just thought this would have been a time his superiors let him stay home. The males here are so protective of their females, you know," she murmured.

Saroya nodded, that familiar pain settling in her chest. She'd never told anyone that her joining with Gage and Linc had really only been a true joining with Gage. Not even Leilani and not Brianna, the two females she'd bonded with on the rescue ships that had brought them to Lumineta. . It didn't matter that she was officially bonded to them both, she'd only slept with Gage.

Leaning forward, Saroya cleared her throat. "Can I tell you something?" she whispered, needing to get this off her chest. Since her friend Brianna had been having a hard time adjusting to all of Lumineta's customs she'd never opened up to her about what things were like at her home. But Leilani loved it here. She might not have chosen mates but that was because she was busy with her job and the woman had made it clear she was picky.

"Of course, what..." She trailed off as her gaze landed behind Saroya. Her pretty lips pulled into a tight line.

Two males approached their table. She and Leilani were sitting outside in a courtyard of the Venesian restaurant they'd chosen, which in hindsight, they probably should have gotten a seat inside of. On Lumineta, she'd quickly come to learn that females out dining by themselves were a rarity. They usually brought a male with them for this very reason. Crime here was almost non-existent and males were respectful of females but . . . they weren't going to pass up approaching two unattached females. Which was going to make talking to her friend impossible tonight. Saroya bit back a frustrated sigh.

Before the two males could stay anything though, Leilani smiled brightly and shook her head. "We're waiting for our mates."

Just like that, the males nodded politely—both looking disappointed—and continued down the street. Saroya snickered under her breath. "Maybe we should just get a plaque made that says that."

"Right? Back to what you were saying." Leilani gave Saroya her full attention then, one of the reasons she adored the other woman.

She knew her friend wouldn't judge her but, still, it was hard to get the words out. *Screw it.* "Linc and I have never slept together." Her voice was barely a whisper. Leilani's dark eyes widened but before she could respond, Saroya continued. "I know I legally joined with both of them but just Gage and I were intimate. I've never slept with Linc," she said even more softly. "Linc said he didn't want to bring anyone else into our house or anything now, but…" She shrugged. "I don't know if he likes women."

Leilani was silent for a long moment, just looking at Saroya in a state of almost shock and horror. Okay, her little confession wasn't *that* bad.

When her friend finally spoke, her words confused Saroya. "Linc is definitely interested in women."

"How do you know that?" she snapped, a surge of anger unexpectedly punctuating her words.

Leilani blinked once in confusion before a wide grin spread across her face. "I *know* because I've seen the way he looks at you. Don't take this the wrong way because it's not like I sit around and fantasize about my best friend, but I used to think you had this epic sex life with the two of them. The way they'd both look at you when you were all together. Yeah, I noticed that Gage was the only one who was affectionate but I just thought Linc wasn't into PDA or something. But he definitely wants you. I've *seen* the way he looks at you and it's hot."

Saroya sat back against her seat, digesting her friend's words. Before Gage died she'd only been with him for six moon cycles and in public both males had always been attentive to her, making it clear she was taken. Linc had never been affectionate, as her friend had noticed, but he'd always been kind. Maybe that was Leilani had seen between the three of him. "You're sure?" She knew how Linc was in private: completely oblivious of her. Maybe Leilani was onto something or maybe she'd just been reading him wrong.

"Oh yeah. No doubt in my mind."

"Then how do I get him to notice me?" she blurted, feeling foolish. It wasn't as if the man was even around for her to do anything with, but he had to return home sometime. He was actually scheduled to be home in a week so maybe she could feel him out then. Or if the opportunity arose, maybe she could make a move. She bit her lip at that thought. She wasn't normally bold but she could make an exception with Linc.

Leilani rubbed her hands together gleefully. "We're going to come up with a game plan that guarantees he can't ignore you. It'll involve you being naked, so fair warning."

Saroya's cheeks turned red, but she laughed at her friend's enthusiasm. Moving to a completely new planet and way of life had been hard enough. Especially immersing herself in a new culture where taking two mates was not only accepted but encouraged. She still sometimes fought guilt over that. There were times when she felt so alone, especially lately. It felt so good to finally open up to someone. And just maybe it would make a difference with her interaction with Linc.

Whenever she saw him again.

* * *

Saroya stripped her silky black shift off and draped it on the trunk at the end of her bed. She'd hang it up tomorrow. Without bothering with the cover, she fell on top of it and stretched out. Blindly, she stared at the gauzy white canopy draped above her bedposts. She knew Linc would never enter her chambers without announcing himself. And he'd never do that anyway so she didn't bother with clothes either. As far as she knew, he'd never stepped foot in her room.

Her heart was heavy and confused. Tonight's dinner with Leilani had helped put things in perspective and reminded her that she wasn't alone, that there were other human women dealing with this culture shock too.

Six moon cycles had passed and even though she missed Gage and the friendship they'd shared, she still *wanted* Linc. She was ashamed that she fantasized about him even now. She'd been terrified when she'd first learned of the Luminet custom of two males to every female. It was why she'd aligned herself with Gage so quickly. Only too late she'd realized that they would give females a choice about who they wanted to mate with and that it didn't have to be right away. Gage had been a good mate, and a kind lover, but she hadn't loved him. He'd been more of a friend than anything.

Back then she'd been so scared of their culture. Everything had been so shocking, including the ability to travel through space and the fact that there were many other alien species—that humans were compatible with. When she'd met Linc she'd been nervous but excited.

But he'd never touched her. In the six moon cycles she'd been with his brother and the six moon cycles since then, he'd never once touched her. In fact, he tended to avoid her, which only confused and hurt her. She'd fantasized more than once about what it would feel like to have those big hands on her body.

Caressing her breasts. Between her legs. Would he be gentle? Probably not. Everything about him screamed pure male power. To her surprise, she didn't want gentle. Where Gage had been sweet and caring, their relationship had not been particularly passionate. She'd never initiated sex between them. Had always let him come to her. And she had a feeling he'd known why.

Her hand strayed between her legs. Maybe it was wrong to think about Linc while she touched herself but she couldn't help it. Even though her mourning period was officially over she'd been emotional and lonely for a while. She wanted to feel release and get some sleep.

Spreading her legs, she lightly touched her clit. It pulsed under her finger. Stroking farther down, she rubbed her slit but didn't penetrate. Just touched.

And imagined.

What would it be like for Linc to feel her there? With his fingers, his tongue…his cock. She'd seen him shirtless before but he'd never allowed her to see more than that. He'd been on a space mission the past three moon cycles and even before that he'd been virtually absent in their home. It was almost as if she lived by herself and she was tired of it. At least she could use the memory of his broad, muscular chest as a starting point for her fantasy.

Using her wetness she strayed up to her clit and slowly circled it with her finger. Her orgasms were never spectacular when she masturbated but the release would help her sleep. After a few torturous days of tossing and turning, Goddess knew she needed it.

As she stroked herself, the door flew open. Her eyes widened as they locked with Linc's dark, equally surprised gaze. Apparently he was back from his mission early.

His stare tracked over her naked body with slow precision. He lifted one muscular arm and rubbed a hand over his dark buzz cut but he didn't stop staring. He paused at her breasts then continued until he stopped at the juncture between her legs. His mouth parted slightly and he sucked in a sharp breath. A forbidden shaft of erotic pleasure speared her. He liked what he saw.

Instead of pulling her hand away, she continued touching herself in slow, even strokes. When she did, his gaze snapped back to hers. His expression was full of confusion and heat. Raw, unbridled desire. But just as quickly, he glanced away and started to shut the door.

"Don't go." The whispered words were out before she realized she'd spoken. She didn't know if she should feel bad about doing this. According to his culture, they should already be sharing a bed. A twinge of guilt lanced through her, but she needed to feel Linc's strength tonight. She was tired of being alone. After her talk with Leilani she was feeling brave. Maybe Linc really was attracted to her.

When he didn't make a move toward her she figured she'd have to take the first step. She pushed up and off the bed and strode toward him, even though she felt exposed and vulnerable. Her movements were unhurried. As he drank in the sight of her, her nipples hardened under his intense scrutiny. She could tell he wanted her. For the first time since they'd met, she could see it written on his face clearly. But she was worried about his rejection.

When she stood in front of him, she reached up and traced her fingers over the scar that crossed his eye, over his cheekbone and all the way down to his square jaw. He always tried to hide that side of his face from people but she didn't know why. He was a warrior and should be proud. Even if he hadn't been on the mission that had saved her and her people, all Luminet warriors were brave, if a little intimidating. They looked like throwbacks to a different time. They dressed similar to the Vikings she'd read about from her history.

He captured her wrist in a dominating grip and held fast. "What the devil are you doing?" His voice was unsteady.

She stared into his obsidian eyes and forgot to breathe. The dark, dangerous vibe he emanated was powerful and incredibly sexual. How many times had she fantasized about being so close to him? She reached out another hand and traced it along his jaw. There was a slight rasp of stubble even though she guessed he'd shaved that morning.

He encircled her other wrist, forcing her to look at him. "Saroya?"

That deep voice was scorching. It made her already hard nipples tingle in awareness. "What did you say?" she murmured.

"What. Are. You. Doing?" His voice was clipped yet strained.

She frowned at him and tried to tug her hands free. If she needed to explain it then obviously he didn't want her the way she'd thought. Her cheeks burned in embarrassment as she wished the floor would just swallow her whole. "Let me go."

Instead, he pulled her until she was flush against him. His erection was hard and hot against her even through his trousers.

"You think I'll throw you out now that the mourning period is over? Even I'm not that much of an animal." His laugh was harsh and dry. "Not that you'd have much trouble finding someone to mate. You *must* know that." He dragged her even harder against him. His hard length insistently stabbed her abdomen.

She didn't understand why he seemed upset but she slipped her arms around his neck and savored the feel of his erection and hard body. "I don't understand what you're saying," she whispered as she focused on his lips.

"You don't have to use your body in exchange for my protection. Something you should know by now." His voice was filled with disgust. Abruptly he stepped back and was gone before she could blink.

Her door shut with a quiet click and a slow building fury grew inside her as she finally digested his words. He thought she was trying to use her body to get him to what, keep or protect her? She had no problem being on her own. And it wasn't arrogant but she knew she'd have no problem finding another male—males—if she wanted to. But she didn't. She just wanted Linc.

Which was just plain stupid considering he thought so little of her. Tears burned her eyes, but she batted them away. She wasn't going to cry over him. No, it was time to move on. Her living here wasn't healthy for either of them. He deserved his own space, not to have to share it with someone who he apparently couldn't stand.

Tomorrow she'd figure out a plan for where she could go.

CHAPTER TWO

Linc slammed his sparring stick across an android's middle, then whirled and sliced at another's throat. Sweat poured down his neck, back and chest as he swiveled again, taking on the third opponent.

He'd come to the Samio hours earlier, needing to blow off steam before anyone else arrived. As one of the senior trainers, he needed to keep a level head at all times. Neither his students nor other warriors needed to see him off his game.

Or out of control. Which is how he felt after last night. The shock and hurt on Saroya's face before he'd left her room still pierced him deep. He'd been cruel and the more he thought about it, the more he wondered if he'd misread her intentions.

Slam.

One of the androids got a hit in with a short wooden dagger, ricocheting off his shoulder. Ducking and turning, he jabbed the stick into its middle, earning another kill point. If he'd been in actual one-on-one battle he'd be using a pulse gun or dagger. But training wasn't about just stopping an opponent and keeping him down, it was about honing their fighting skills and staying sharp, ready for any attack.

Their planet was peaceful but they had occasional skirmishes with off-worlders looking to expand their territory. Most of their battles were from one of their ships, but from the age of ten all Luminet males joined the Samio and began their battle-training.

Just as he swiped one of the android's legs out from under it, the three machines jerked to a halt.

"You trying to actually kill those thing?" A male voice asked.

Linc turned to find Aeron standing against the weapons center wall, his hand on the stop button for the androids. Next to him, all sorts of weapons covered the wall: knives, pulse guns, daggers, and sparring sticks. "Just getting in some early training."

Aeron nodded and crossed the light blue mat toward him. "How are things with you and Saroya?"

The abrupt question made Linc bristle. "How is that your concern?" He was friends with the other warrior and respected him, but he also knew that Aeron and his brother Hauk were looking for a new mate after theirs died.

Aeron paused for a moment, but continued. The tall blond male stopped when he was in front of him. "I know what it is like to lose someone. I know you still have Saroya but Gage was your brother. I can't imagine losing Hauk."

Linc's throat grew tight. He still missed Gage, even as he lusted after Saroya. "Things have been difficult." He didn't plan to open up to anyone about his relationship with Saroya. The shame was too great. He should be with her right now and if her reaction to him last night was any indication, he could have been with her that very moment. Or at least leaving her bed and getting ready for work. Instead he was here sweating his balls off and frustrated.

"That's understandable, especially with your schedule. I know it is not my place, but as a friend, maybe if you refused your next mission, you'd be able to spend more time with Saroya. The distance between you two must be hard on her."

Linc just nodded. He actually hadn't been assigned his last mission, he'd volunteered for it. Being under the same roof as Saroya was getting harder and harder. And now that he'd seen her naked, touching herself . . . fuck. He rubbed a hand over his face. That image was seared into his mind.

As he'd jerked off in the shower last night—then again this morning—all he'd been able to see was her flat on her back, slender legs spread wide as she stroked between her folds.

He still couldn't believe she hadn't stopped when he'd walked in on her. That she'd continued, watching him, her eyes inviting him to join her. Then she'd actually *asked* him to join her.

All the muscles in his body pulled taut at the memory. God, then he'd insulted her instead of taking her into his arms like he'd been fantasizing about. He wanted her, but he couldn't be a replacement for his brother, someone she just turned to for comfort.

"Thank you for the advice," he said belatedly, not wanting to insult his friend. He knew Aeron meant well.

"Any time. Maybe you will put in a good word for me with Brianna?" Aeron's gaze was hopeful.

Linc found himself smiling. "You're still after her?"

The other warrior nodded once. "She will be our mate. You'll see."

Linc didn't respond. The redheaded human was one of Saroya's friends and had always been a good friend to her. Something that made him automatically like her. Her kindness was apparent, but he'd heard her tell Saroya more than once that she wasn't sure if she could take two mates. The planet they came from was so different than Lumineta in so many ways.

"Would you like a real sparring partner before the students arrive? Unless you like beating on defenseless robots." Aeron turned back toward the weapons wall, already knowing Linc's answer would be yes.

Especially today when he was so wound up he knew that nothing short of a marathon of sex with Saroya would tame all his energy. Since that wasn't happening, fighting would have to do.

* * *

Saroya slid the leftovers from the evening meal into the cooler as Brianna sat at the island in the kitchen.

"Thanks for having me over," Brianna said. "I've really missed you the past couple weeks."

Saroya turned and leaned against the counter, smiling. "I've missed you too." And it was good getting back into a routine. During her mourning period she hadn't taught many art classes, but she'd desperately missed it. Luckily now that the official time was over it didn't look strange to anyone that she was taking on a full load of classes again. She wouldn't have minded teaching them before, but she'd been afraid of insulting anyone. This new culture was tricky.

"Do you have any dessert hiding in there?" Brianna's eyebrows rose as she nodded at the cooler.

"I might have ordered triple-layer suklaada—" She nearly jumped at the sound of the transport platform in the connecting living room beeping. The whooshing sound made her nearly lose her breath. No one but Linc and her were programmed into the system so she knew it was him arriving.

A second later he strode by the kitchen and paused when he saw her and Brianna.

"Hey, Linc. We're just about to have dessert. Want to join us?" Brianna said, smiling.

Linc looked at Saroya and she felt her face flame as she thought of last night. It almost looked as if he was asking her if she wanted to join him so she forced her vocal chords to work. "Yes, I'm sorry you missed the evening meal but please join us." Goddess, she sounded all formal and ridiculous.

Nodding, he stepped carefully into the room, as if he was afraid she might bite. Surprising, considering what he'd said last night. Last night she'd been so ready to move on and get out of here after his hurtful words, but the more she thought about it, the more she wondered if he'd thought she just wanted to use him. Until last night she'd never come out and made her feelings clear so she might need to be more blunt.

Luminet males were so confusing so she simply wasn't sure. Thinking of Leilani's advice, she decided she'd try.

"I saw Aeron today, he asked about you," Linc said to Brianna.

Brianna snorted as Saroya turned her back to them and started pulling the cake out. The triple-layer dessert was sweet, rich and to die for. She put pieces on two plates, half-listening as Brianna and Linc talked about Aeron and his persistence.

When she approached the island Linc started to stand for her, but she shook her head. "We can share," she said, sliding a small plate to Brianna.

It was a normal custom for couples or trios to share or even for males to feed females. She'd never let Gage do that because it seemed weird, but she didn't mind sharing with Linc.

Linc's dark eyes were unreadable as he watched her move closer to him, tracking her every step.

The tunic he wore today had three-quarter inch length sleeves, showing off his muscular, tattooed forearms. And his scent, all spicy and wild, only added to the raw, untamed package of Linc. Everything about him was simply so male it made her crazy. He was so very different from Gage too.

Instead of sitting next to him, she moved so that she was half in between his legs. According to Luminet customs females often sat in one of their males' laps during desserts or after dinner drinks. Sometimes she'd done it with Gage, but never Linc.

Still, he knew what she was silently asking. Brianna wouldn't think anything of it, not when she understood the customs. Maybe if Saroya showed him that she wasn't using him, that she was proud to call him her mate, he'd understand. Maybe not, but it was a start. She felt like she was treading deep water with him, trying to figure the confusing male out.

Thankfully he didn't embarrass her, but easily scooped her up and into his lap. She sat sideways on his thighs, her legs draped over him. He wrapped one of his big arms around her so that his hand settled firmly on her hip, holding her tight in place. It felt almost possessive, but she wondered if that was just her imagination going wild. More than anything, it felt natural.

Just like that, her body lit on fire, her core flooding with a rush of heat. They'd never sat so intimately before.

"You guys are so sweet," Brianna murmured. "So are you back for a while? You've been gone for so long," she said to Linc.

Saroya picked up her fork and cut off a small bite as Linc answered.

"Not sure yet."

"Oh, well, I hope you don't have to run off again so quickly. I know Saroya misses you," Brianna said before taking another bite.

"Is that right?" he murmured, for her ears only, leaning closer so that his nose was nearly touching her upper jaw and ear.

His erection was unmistakable, hard and insistent against her, giving her hope that there could be something between them.

For a brief moment Saroya wondered if he'd nip her earlobe. She knew he actually wouldn't, not in front of company, but her nipples hardened in anticipation just the same.

"Yes," she managed to rasp out when his hand tightened on her hip. She could feel her heart beating overtime, the staccato thump so out of control she knew he had to hear it too. She wished her friend was gone and that she and Linc were all alone.

Suddenly, the comm unit on his belt beeped and he jerked back. He still held onto her hip, but whatever had been happening, or not happening, between them, was over.

He looked at the hand-held device and frowned. "I need to take this. It's the Samio." His grip on her hip increased for a second before he gently slid her off his lap and made apologies to Brianna for having to take his call.

As soon as he'd gone to his room, Saroya's heart rate returned to normal and she managed to hold a normal conversation with Brianna for another hour.

Linc never returned and even another hour after her friend had gone home, he still hadn't come out of his room.

That was when she realized he wasn't coming out at all. She briefly thought about going to his room, but after his blunt rejection last night wasn't sure her pride could take another one. Sighing, she knew she needed to just make the hard decision and move out. It was time to move on. Just because she turned him didn't mean anything. Because she wanted more than just sex—not that he was even offering.

CHAPTER THREE

Saroya rubbed a hand over the back of her neck, beyond exhausted after the day she'd had. After a full load of classes, she just wanted to collapse with a glass of *villana*. All day she'd been dreading telling Linc she'd be moving out.

She still wasn't sure how the logistics would work, especially since her studio was on his property. Or her property too, she guessed. She knew she had all sorts of legal rights, which was good. But right now it felt like just more stuff to worry about. Goddess, her head hurt even thinking about it. As she strode down the hallway toward the kitchen, she tightened her silk robe tighter around her. It was already late so she guessed she wouldn't get the chance to tell Linc tonight.

Part of her wondered why his leaders made him work such long hours. He was a senior officer so she'd assumed he'd have some sort of seniority or privileges. Gage had worked hard, but he certainly hadn't worked the exceedingly long hours Linc did.

As she reached the end of the hallway, the transport platform beeped then whooshed. Wasn't that just perfect timing. With nowhere to go, she wrapped her arms around her middle as Linc appeared.

He blinked once when he saw her standing by the hallway entryway, clearly surprised to see her.

"I was just..." She cleared her throat. He didn't need to know she was going to the kitchen, he didn't need to know anything about what she was going because he obviously didn't care. "Listen, I hate the way things have been going between us and I really hate feeling like I'm invading your space all the time. I'm going to be moving out. I still need to figure out some stuff, but I promise it'll be as soon as I possibly can." Maybe that would ease the tension between them.

His jaw tightened as he stepped off the platform and moved toward her. Today he wore a simple tunic and loose pants, the style that was so standard of the males of the planet. "Moving out?" For some reason he sounded stunned.

She couldn't imagine why. "I think it will be for the best."

He just watched her steadily for a moment, his gaze intent and searching. Then that annoyingly sexy jaw of his tightened and he just nodded and muttered a 'fine' before hurriedly moving past her. Her gaze dropped as he did and she realized he was rock hard. Her eyes widened. What the hell? Was that for her? Before Gage she hadn't had much experience with men and definitely not one with social interactions on her planet. Every day had been a fight for survival against the elements or other people. Now she really wished she understood males more.

She thought about returning to her room, but Linc's non-response angered her. As the sharp burst of annoyance simmered inside her, she stalked down to his room. The stone steps were so cold—the whole damn house always seemed cold—so she picked up her pace. Maybe she should just cut her losses and leave but she was so far beyond that.

Without bothering to knock she shoved his door open. He sat on the edge of the huge bed, his face buried in his hands. He jerked up when he saw her.

"Did I do something to offend you? Or is it just my presence in general?" she demanded, needing to understand his reaction to her.

"No." His voice was hoarse.

"I don't understand you, Linc. I didn't think you even wanted me, then . . . well, last night I felt your reaction on my hip and then just now I saw . . . I don't think you were faking that reaction, were you?" She really wished she understood males—or just him—more.

His jaw hardened. "No."

"Then why did you push me away? Do you really want me gone?"

"*No.* I just . . . I don't want you coming to me because you think you need protection. I know your official mourning period is over and I don't want you to think you have to do this," he muttered. He rubbed his hand over his buzz cut and let out a string of curses.

She frowned. "Protection? I *want* you, Linc. In my bed. That's all. I thought I made that clear the other night." But maybe she hadn't.

When he just stared at her, she was suddenly aware of how little clothing she had on. The robe covered her, but it molded to her curves and under his hot gaze, she might as well be nude. She wrapped her arms around her chest and took a small step back. Maybe this had been a huge mistake. Before she could take another step, he'd crossed the room and his hands tightly gripped her hips.

His dark eyes seared hers. "If you let me in your bed, I'm not leaving."

She nodded as the heat inside her built again. A deep throb pulsed between her legs.

"*Ever.* Do you understand?"

She nodded again because she didn't trust her voice. This is what she'd always wanted from him. It felt too surreal that he was actually making a move.

"And we're not bringing anyone else into this bed." The possessive note in his voice made her toes curl.

Something primal inside her she'd forgotten existed flared to life. She could feel years of evolution being stripped away as he devoured her with his eyes. She'd always wanted to welcome him into the bedroom with her and Gage, but with Linc staring at her now, she didn't want anyone else to touch her. "I understand."

Linc couldn't believe Saroya stood in front of him offering herself and he wasn't going to pass up this opportunity. Part of him wondered if she was using him as a way to get over her grief. She'd had time to mourn but the woman was very guarded sometimes. It might be selfish to take advantage of her vulnerability but he didn't care. She'd already shown him more than once that she was willing and he just wanted her. Wanted to sink inside her and lose himself for hours. He was starving for her touch, for the comfort only she could give.

With trembling hands he reached for her robe and pulled it open. She tensed for a moment but when he pushed the silky material off her shoulders, she let out a long breath.

Her hard nipples and erratic breathing spoke volumes. She wanted him. Even if she tried to deny it, she couldn't.

His erection felt like a heavy club between his legs. Every instinct he possessed told him to take her fast and hard. To rut like an animal. The fear of hurting her was the only thing that made him hold back.

Her long, dark hair fell over her shoulders in soft waves. The locks fell on either side of her breasts, framing her perfection. As he drank in the sight of her, his hips jerked toward her with insistency. Yeah, his dick had a mind of its own.

Before he could change his mind, not that there was ever much fear of that happening, he covered her mouth with his.

His kisses were forceful, demanding, and she returned them with equal urgency. Her almost frenzied state surprised him. She tasted sweet, better than he'd fantasized about. Her hands dug into his shoulders and as their tongues danced, she moaned into his mouth.

The moan was what set him off. Still holding her hips—maybe out of fear she'd change her mind—he lifted her and carried her to his bed. A place he'd never thought to see her. So many times he'd thought about seeking her out but it had always seemed too soon to make a move. Seeing her touching herself the other night and the way she'd willingly searched him out was too much to ignore.

Though he loathed tearing his mouth away from hers, he deposited her onto the bed. He tried to be gentle but it was hard when he had her naked and willing in front of him.

She didn't stay on her back. Sitting up, she grasped his belt and fumbled with it. He could have stared all day watching her try to rip his clothes off but that would mean he wouldn't get to feel her naked body against his.

As she worked to get it free he grabbed his tunic and peeled it off. When he did she paused and stared at his chest.

Something inside him swelled as her mouth dropped open slightly. She stared at him unabashedly and with complete hunger. The pulse point in her neck increased wildly. When she ran her tongue over her lips, his cock jumped.

He needed inside her.

Now.

Without wasting any more time he covered her mouth with his once again. She let out a surprised yelp as he pinned her to the bed and it only made him hotter. As he covered her body with his, he shimmied out of his trousers.

Once his erection rubbed against her bare mound he growled. The sound was primal and tore from him unexpectedly. The feel of her soft, welcoming folds against him was too much.

He, who was known for his stamina, wasn't going to last long before he came.

Saroya arched her back, rubbing her soft breasts over his chest. The feel of her hard nipples made him ache all over. His cock throbbed between his legs. If he didn't get in her, he feared he'd come on her stomach.

That thought brought up horror inside him. A tiny voice in his head told him to give her foreplay but he couldn't. Something primal in him worried she'd change her mind. Tell him this was all a mistake.

With a low growl, Linc grabbed her hips and plunged inside her. She was wet and very willing but so fucking tight.

Saroya's eyes widened and she expelled a small gasp as he filled her. Her inner walls expanded and molded around him. For a moment her breathing was shallow and erratic.

Instead of pulling out and slamming back into her as his body demanded, he held very still. *Shit.* Had he fucked up or what. He should have tested her slickness. Played with her clit until she was ready. What kind of animal was he?

Her legs widened around him and for an agonizing moment he thought she was going to push him away. Instead, she wrapped her legs around his waist and rolled her hips. She moaned softly as he pushed into her again.

Linc lost it.

The harder he moved in her, the louder she cried out. His brain threatened to short circuit at those damn sounds.

After covering her mouth again, his tongue danced and intertwined with hers in a way he'd only dreamed about. There was nothing soft or delicate about the way she returned his kisses.

As he moved in and out of her, she dug her fingers into his back and held fast. With each pump into her, his ball sac pulled up tighter. The feel of her tight walls gripping him, holding him, was too much. She milked him harder and harder until he couldn't restrain himself any longer.

Holding back a cry, he emptied himself into Saroya. Spilling his seed into her filled him with a pleasure he didn't understand.

But there was one thing he knew. She hadn't come with him. Breathing raggedly, he lifted his head from her shoulder and stared into her blue eyes.

At least he was still hard inside her. For how he felt, his erection would never soften again. "I'm sorry," he whispered. In all his fantasies, making her climax had been his number one goal.

Her smile was soft, understanding, and it pissed him off. She should be reaming him out for treating her so roughly and not taking care of her first. He'd never felt like more of a barbarian than he did in that moment. But he intended to make it up to her.

Staying deep inside her, he reached between them and ran his thumb around her clit. When he did, her eyes glazed over slightly.

"Tell me what you like," he murmured.

"This. I like this." Her eyes were closed and her voice unsteady.

As he teased and tweaked her clit, he began moving inside her again. This time his movements were slow, steady, and by the feel of her inner walls contracting, exactly what she wanted.

She tightened with each flick over her sensitive bundle of nerves. Watching the pleasure play across her face made him ache. He could watch her until she came but he desperately wanted to kiss all of her.

Keeping his movements even, he leaned down and grasped one of her pink nipples between his teeth.

She jerked at the tugging action. Worried he'd hurt her, he stopped, but when he saw the erotic expression on her face, all his concern disappeared.

"Don't stop. I like that." Her words were barely a whisper.

Switching breasts, he kissed and licked her other nipple before tugging on it. Her entire body reacted to the caresses. Her back arched and her vagina tightened around him in rapid contractions.

The little vixen was definitely sensitive there. He continued his assault of teasing her nipples then blowing on the moist, hardened buds while he strummed her clit.

He could feel how close she was. Her body was tense and primed and ready to come. Somehow he knew she was holding back, though he didn't know why.

Shifting forward, he leaned close to her ear. When he did, she wrapped both her arms around him, her fingers digging into his back.

"Come for me," he whispered and simultaneously pinched her clit. Not hard, but with enough pressure to push her over the edge.

"Linc." She moaned his name as her inner walls tightened around his hard length. She milked him as her climax tore through her with no restraint. When she moaned his name again he thrust harder and faster.

He hadn't thought it possible but another orgasm roared through him. Not as powerful as before but with startling intensity.

As they both rode through the waves of their climax, he finally collapsed on top of her. Using his elbows to prop himself up, he hovered above her.

Saroya's bright blue eyes were wide with almost wonderment. As if she couldn't believe what they'd just done. His throat seized at the thought that she might regret it.

Carefully he eased out of her even though it was the last thing he wanted to do. They were both sticky and he knew she'd want to clean up but for now he just wanted to be close to her. He stretched out next to her and placed a hand on her flat abdomen. For only a moment her muscles clenched then relaxed under his touch. She hadn't said anything or made a move to leave and her breathing was still erratic and shaky. The silence wasn't uncomfortable but he still wanted to hear her voice.

In the short amount of time she'd lived with them she hadn't slept in his brother's room. He hated that he'd noticed or cared. But he had. She'd always returned to her room on the nights they'd been . . . together. Something he shouldn't be thinking about. It would only torture him.

"Stay with me tonight." The words were out before he could stop himself.

She rolled on her side to face him and smiled. Reaching out, she placed her hand on his chest and stroked her fingers over his taut skin. "Okay."

That word was all he needed to hear. They weren't done for the night. Not by a long shot. He'd wanted to get her in this position for too long and he wasn't going to waste the opportunity. By the time the night was through he planned to kiss, taste and touch every inch of her.

CHAPTER FOUR

Saroya stretched her arms above her head before opening her eyes. As she glanced around the room she realized Linc was gone. She reached out and touched his side of the bed. If she had to guess she'd say he'd left a while ago because it wasn't warm.

She'd known he had training today but she'd expected him to wake her up to say goodbye or…something. After the night they'd shared she'd thought things would be different between them. A hollow ache settled in her chest.

Shoving aside her hurt, she got out of bed. Dwelling on it wouldn't do her any good. The instant her feet touched the stone floor she realized how stiff she was. Her entire body was sore.

A good sore, but she'd be feeling Linc all over her the entire day. He'd been a machine last night. She didn't even remember falling asleep. They'd rested after the first time but he'd been insatiable.

Hungry and lusty and exactly what she'd needed. No man had ever touched her the way he had. The last time he'd taken her from behind and he'd actually nibbled and lightly bit her neck. Like he was claiming her. The action had pushed her into another orgasm. Thinking about it, she reached up and lightly rubbed the tender spot.

He might not have talked a lot, but for how talented he was with his mouth and hands, he didn't have to. That didn't explain why he hadn't woken her to say goodbye this morning.

She hated that it bothered her so much. The way he'd held her and taken her, she'd never experienced such a heated coupling. A shiver rolled through her and she forced herself to move toward the shower. Instead of taking one in his room she returned to hers and quickly got ready.

Even though she was tired, she still had to teach today. Her students were at that perfect age where none of the boys had gone to Samio training yet. When they turned ten all males were sent to what basically amounted to warrior training.

While she'd come to love Lumineta, it was a planet full of warriors and it had taken some getting used to. She'd seen enough war and violence during her twenty-eight years on her home planet to last four lifetimes. Natural disasters had rocked her entire planet over and over and if that wasn't enough, her people had destroyed almost all their natural resources. If it hadn't been for the Luminet warriors on a scouting mission, she and her band of friends would have died.

Thankfully the Luminet warriors treated all people with respect and didn't go out of their way to start wars. But they protected their unique planet with twelve moons and their limited number of females with a vengeance.

After showering and dressing she didn't bother using the transport platform. Her studio and classrooms were behind the house in one giant building. Something Linc had actually had built for her. Gage had told her later that it had been his brother's idea to let her teach art to the younger members of their clan and he'd convinced their leader to give her permission. She even had a few students from one of the mountain clans sign up this moon cycle.

The moment she entered her classroom, she smiled. Seeing the ten students in her first class already waiting in front of their easels instantly brightened her dark mood. If she'd stayed home, she'd have definitely gone mad.

The day went by in a blur. One class blended into the next until she found herself rinsing out her brushes alone and dreaming of putting her feet up and letting Linc have it for leaving this morning the way he had. The more she thought about the way he'd practically sneaked out, the angrier she got.

A sharp knock at her door startled her. When she turned, she found Aeron, another warrior, taking a tentative step into the room. The tall, muscular blond was a little bigger than Linc, maybe six foot seven, though somehow more approachable. He definitely had that warrior thing going on but his young son was in her class and she genuinely liked him.

"Hi, Aeron. Finn left a while ago," she said, referring to his son. On Lumineta there wasn't much crime and children traveled through the transport pods or shuttles freely. She turned off the water valve and wiped her hands on her paint-stained apron.

"I know. I came to see you." His dark eyes were unreadable and his face impassive.

"Ah, okay. Want to walk me home?"

He nodded stiffly, as if he was uncomfortable being here, then moved back so she could pass him. Once outside a cool breeze rolled over them. Where they lived it was lush and warm year round and the wind was always welcome.

When he still hadn't spoken, she glanced at him. "Are you going to say what you came to say or make me play the question game?"

He cleared his throat, a smile playing at his lips. "Are you doing okay? I know your mourning period is officially over."

She didn't know him well enough to discuss her feelings with him. "Is that why you came to see me? To check on me?"

He shook his head as they reached the back door of the house. Clearing his throat again, he looked suddenly nervous. "You're friends with Brianna?" He formed it as a question even though he knew she was close with the redhead.

Saroya nodded, suddenly understanding where he was headed. "Yes."

"My brother and I are looking to take a mate and—"

"She's not interested?" She already knew what he was going to say before he said it.

He nodded. "Yes. We've both tried to visit her, court her, but she refuses both of us. I know . . . that she is attracted to me and she doesn't act like she's interested in anyone else. I don't know what to do to convince her we are serious about her."

"I don't doubt she knows you're serious. That might be the problem."

He frowned at her.

Saroya tried to find the right words. "You and your brother want a mate but you also have a son. I don't know, but she might not want to be just a substitute for your deceased mate or even a mother, or…it's possible she doesn't want to be with two warriors."

"Why wouldn't she?" He stared at her incredulously.

Saroya sighed. Not all of the women who'd been saved from her planet had adjusted to the cultural differences and Aeron didn't seem to understand that. She tried to take a different approach. "Have you thought about starting off casual first?" Because the male was right, Brianna was definitely attracted to Aeron. Her friend had told her that more than once. It was the cultural differences that scared her.

His scowl deepened. "Casual? I don't *want* anything casual with her. And she would never be a substitute." His words had more force than she expected.

Saroya bit back a smile because she knew he wouldn't appreciate it. Many Luminet males were similar in that manner. When they wanted something, they went after it with single-minded determination. She'd seen more than one of her friends succumb to the charms of Luminet warriors. Even though she'd been happy for her friends she'd always felt a sadness that Linc had never wanted her. Until last night anyway. She shook those thoughts away and focused on the man in front of her. "What I'm trying to say is be more subtle in your approach with her."

His expression darkened, as if the word was foreign. "Subtle?"

"Yes. *Subtle.*"

"Huh." He slowly nodded. "Okay, subtle. Thank you."

"You're welcome. Do you need to use the transport platform inside?" She motioned with her hand toward the back door.

He shook his head. "No, I took a shuttle." Surprising her, he reached out and cupped her cheek.

She nearly jerked back until she realized what he was doing.

"You've got a couple smudges of paint," he muttered as he swiped his thumb across her cheekbone.

The touch was completely non-sexual but for some reason she felt odd having anyone but Linc touch her. Which was crazy considering they'd just made love for the first time last night.

"Thanks. I—" Before she could finish Linc appeared from around the side of the house and came at them fast.

He slammed Aeron against the giant wood door and held his arm against his throat. "Touch her again and lose your hand, warrior." The words were said low but she still heard them.

"Linc! He was just wiping paint off my face." She rushed to them and tried to tug on his arm. The man was completely immovable. Like hard steel.

Aeron's face was turning red from the pressure of Linc's arm but he didn't fight back. He nodded once and Linc let him go.

"What is wrong with you, Linc?" She tugged his arm again but he refused to look at her. He still glared daggers at Aeron who hadn't moved from his position by the door.

"He's right, Saroya. I shouldn't have touched you. I apologize, Linc." Aeron held up his hands in a gesture of surrender and raised his eyebrows.

Linc nodded and let him pass, but didn't move from his protective position of Saroya.

"Thank you for the advice, Saroya," Aeron said as he strode around the side of the house.

Finally Linc looked at her and immediately his expression softened. The look took her off guard. "Are you okay?"

She frowned. "Of course I'm okay. What's wrong with you? I thought Aeron was your friend."

His eyes flashed with something dark and predatory. "That doesn't matter. He should not have come to see you without me here and he should not have touched you."

So many moon cycles later and she was still getting used to their customs. "That's the dumbest thing I've heard. And you have a lot of nerve getting mad anyway."

He faltered for a moment. "What do you mean?"

She rolled her eyes to cover the hurt that once again bubbled back up. All day she'd been keeping it at bay but seeing him in the flesh made the hurt reappear. "You sneak away this morning without even waking me up. After the night we shared I expected more than that." She felt foolish admitting it out loud but he'd hurt her feelings and she wanted him to know.

"I didn't want to wake you up."

She glared at him. "That's it?"

His dark eyebrows rose. "What else do you want?"

His non-answer infuriated her. Brushing past him, she tugged open the heavy wood door to their kitchen. She'd planned to make them an evening meal but she needed a few minutes to cool off. She didn't glance at him as she headed for her room. She wasn't going to stand around and argue with him when he'd just acted like a jackass to Aeron then refused to apologize to her. She knew she wasn't crazy for expecting more from him.

Once in her room she balled up her dirty apron and tossed it onto the floor. She couldn't believe he hadn't even acted a little sorry. "I didn't want to wake you up," she muttered in disgust, mimicking him. What a stupid, totally male answer.

"I didn't." She spun around at his deep voice.

"How did you…" She shook her head. The man was very stealth so she didn't bother finishing. "Don't sneak up on me." Instinctively she crossed her arms over her chest. She hadn't heard him enter her chambers and he looked so out of place in the feminine room. Soft, seascape paintings adorned all her sage-colored walls and her furniture was small, white and feminine. The bed was big and fluffy with the canopy decorating it.

He looked around her room curiously for a moment before he returned that hot, dark gaze to hers.

"I was afraid if I woke you up this morning I wouldn't be able to keep my hands off you. Last night I was rough. I didn't want you to think I was some sort of animal. You're right though. I should have said goodbye."

The sincerity of his words softened her anger until it melted away. He was very different from his brother. Something she knew. She couldn't and shouldn't compare them either. Nodding, she kept her gaze on him. "Okay." She had to remind herself that there would be a learning curve for the two of them as they navigated whatever this thing happening between them was.

Immediately the tension in his shoulders fled as he relaxed. "Are you hungry?"

For him. She didn't say it aloud but he must have read the look in her eyes. All day she'd tried to keep him out of her head but seeing him now made her knees weak. Shame filled her that she wasn't mourning Gage more but with Linc so close it was easy to be with him.

"It's been a while and my brother would have wanted you to be happy," he said, as if he understood her fears.

She narrowed her gaze. "How do you know?"

"Because he told me on more than one occasion. We were different in many ways, but what he felt for you was real. He always said that if anything happened to him, he wanted me to take care of you."

A sudden, sickening thought filled her. "Is that why—"

He shook his head sharply, cutting her off. "Don't even go there, Saroya."

The way he said her name made her nipples tingle and the juncture between her thighs ache. There was a predatory gleam in his dark eyes that put her on edge. Like he was ready to pounce. She suddenly felt like he was a hunter and she was his prey. The need to fill the silence between them was overwhelming. "I'd planned to make some *skause* if you're hungry."

Skause was similar to what her people would have considered stew. Of course before her people had been rescued from their dying planet, meat hadn't been an option. She'd had some as a child but as the wars had grown worse, the food supplies had dwindled. On Lumineta, there was an overabundance and tonight she was thankful she could make stew with the proper ingredients.

He nodded, never taking his gaze from hers. Nervous, she wiped her damp palms on her dark shift and glanced at a point over his shoulder. "I should probably get started."

"I'll help you." He followed her to the kitchen. Having him so near was nerve racking.

In the past he'd rarely shown up at home in time for the evening meal and sometimes she hadn't seen Linc for days at a time. That was when he was even on the planet. Gage had always told her he was a workaholic but now she wondered. "Did you not have to work late today?" she asked as she pulled out a big pot from one of the lower cabinets.

His eyebrows drew together as he poured her a glass. "No. I'll probably return home every day at this time."

"Oh." She frowned and pulled out the slab of meat she'd left out to thaw earlier that morning. After grabbing a knife, she started cubing it when he placed a glass of *villana* on the counter next to her.

"Do you have a problem with the time I'm coming home?" There was a trace of something in his voice she couldn't put her finger on. He sounded almost unsure of himself.

She paused to look at him. "No. You just never did in the past. I've barely seen you home for the evening meal in the past twelve moon cycles."

There was a long pause, but finally he spoke. "That will be changing now." His voice had gotten deeper, more sensual.

"You don't have to change your work schedule because of me." Though she really hoped he did.

For a moment he looked confused, then his face turned to an unreadable mask. "When I'm not on missions, I am one of the senior trainers at the Samio."

She frowned at the obvious statement. "I know."

"I make my own schedule and have for a long time." The words hung heavy in the air.

When his meaning sank in she wasn't sure what to do with it. If he made his own schedule he'd been choosing to work late. That meant he'd likely been avoiding her on purpose. She knew she hadn't been paranoid about that. The knowledge hurt her in a way she didn't understand. Even though he hadn't been around much they'd shared a few moments over the past few moon cycles that had been special to her. She didn't respond because she didn't know what to say. Turning away from him, she swallowed hard and tossed the meat into the pot.

As she started to wash her hands, she felt Linc come up behind her before she heard him.

His big hands settled lightly on her hips and he brushed her hair to the side before nuzzling her ear. "Did I say something to upset you?"

She shook her head because she didn't trust her voice. What was there to say anyway?

"Don't lie to me," he murmured before capturing her earlobe between his teeth. When he tugged on it, her knees weakened.

Somehow she found her voice. "You really make your own schedule?"

"Yes." His voice skittered over her skin and she had to grip the sink for support.

"Then why did you usually come home so late before? Is it because…you didn't want to see me?" She wasn't sure why she was asking now, but she needed to know.

Behind her, Linc stiffened and drew back. Instead of answering he pulled away. Immediately she missed his warmth.

"I'll chop up the vegetables for you," he said with no inflection in his voice.

She gritted her teeth but didn't pursue the subject. She didn't plan to let it drop but she didn't have the energy right now to get an answer. The male was so confusing and maddening. If he admitted she was the reason he'd stayed away in the past she didn't know that her heart could take that.

Everything about Linc was so closed off sometimes. Until last night she'd had no idea he was even interested in her. After the many times they'd made love she had no doubt he was attracted to her. But attraction was different than caring for her. Now she wasn't so sure if going to bed with him had been a mistake.

Linc hated the hurt look on Saroya's face and he wasn't sure how to wipe it away. She'd turned away from him again as she stirred vegetables and broth into the pot but he could read the tense lines of her body. The shift she wore today was low cut in the back, revealing soft, smooth skin he wanted to kiss and cover with his hands. That wasn't going to happen any time soon if he didn't get his head out of his ass.

He wanted to answer her truthfully but feared it would hurt her more. He *had* avoided her since she'd moved in with them. Working late had been the only way to avoid awkward interactions. Seeing her and Gage together had torn him apart inside and he wasn't a masochist. His brother had once asked him about his late hours, but he'd brushed him off. Maybe he should have been more honest. But if he had, it wouldn't have changed anything. Saroya and Gage would have still been sleeping together.

"How was your day?" The question came out strained, something she no doubt noticed.

With her back still to him, she shrugged, the action jerky. "Fine. I had a full class schedule."

"The clan is very grateful for what you're doing."

She glanced over her shoulder, an expression of surprise on her pretty face. "Really?"

He nodded. "Orn thinks it's good for the children." Their clan leader was an older warrior and he'd very slowly embraced the abundance of arts and literature the women from the blue planet had brought with them. Linc had eventually convinced him to let Saroya open an art school. Seeing her face when she'd first stepped into her new studio had been worth all the groveling to his leader.

The evening meal went by too quickly. Linc knew she was still upset with him and he didn't know how to make it right. Talking to her was more difficult than he'd counted on. He wished they could just be naked in his bed and not worry about words. Talking was overrated anyway. After they ate he helped her clean up then she disappeared to her room.

After a few hours passed and he waited in his bed alone, his annoyance and lust grew. Last night he'd told her he wouldn't be leaving her bed and he'd meant it.

CHAPTER FIVE

Saroya curled up on her bed and blindly watched the video screen on her wall. No rain and sunny skies for tomorrow. Not that she particularly cared. All she could think about was Linc. He'd basically admitted he'd been avoiding her for months and she didn't understand why. After the evening meal she'd felt awkward and tongue-tied and he hadn't helped in the conversation department any so she'd left, showered, and climbed into bed.

She'd thought about going to his bedroom but in the end decided against it. Sighing, she clicked off the vid screen then used voice command to dim the lights in her room.

As she lay back against her pillow, her door creaked open. Immediately she pushed up and her breath caught in her throat.

Linc stood in the doorway, his broad frame filling it almost completely. From the light in the hallway and the streams of moonlight coming through her windows, she could see he wasn't wearing a tunic. Just loose trousers that looked like his training pants. When he silently stepped farther into the room, the anger on his face was evident.

She wasn't scared he'd hurt her, but a sudden burst of alarm surged through her. "What are you doing?"

"I think I should be asking you the same thing," he growled softly.

"Excuse me?" She pulled her sheet higher over her breasts. She usually slept naked but now that Linc had taken to entering her room without knocking she might change the practice.

"I told you once you let me into your bed I wouldn't be leaving it." He strode toward the other side of the bed, then to her surprise he slipped in next to her. Lying on his back, he closed his eyes and had the nerve to look completely at ease. As if he had every right to be there.

Her gaze strayed to his bare chest. All those muscular lines and striations just begged to be touched, kissed, but he was crazy if he thought she'd be sleeping with him tonight.

Of course, he looked like he had every intention of just *sleeping*. It shouldn't annoy her, but it did. Very much so.

"What do you think you're doing?" she demanded.

"What does it look like?" He didn't open his eyes, which infuriated her.

She gritted her teeth. "You can't just...get into my bed like this."

A ghost of a smile played across his face. "I already have," he murmured.

Saroya sat there for a long moment, watching him, sure he'd move or something. Nothing. Feeling restless by his relaxed state, she decided to grab some water. She threw off the sheet and started to get out of bed. Before her feet touched the ground his hand snaked around her waist and pulled her back. In seconds he had her pinned under him.

And he was rock-hard all over. His covered length rubbed against her folds as he settled on top of her. Caging her in with his hands on either side of her head, he stared down at her intently.

His dark eyes seemed fathomless in the dim light. "We either sleep in your bed or mine, but we sleep together."

"But why? You basically admitted you've been avoiding me the past six moon cycles. Longer even! What am I even supposed to say to that? You haven't wanted to be around me and now all of a sudden you're changing your schedule. I don't understand you, Linc. After last night I know you want me, but—"

"I avoided you because if I didn't I knew I wouldn't keep my hands off you!" The abrupt declaration stunned her.

A dozen questions rolled around in her head but only one formed on her lips. "Why did you stop yourself?" she whispered.

His jaw clenched tightly. She didn't think he'd answer but finally he spoke. "The thought of seeing another man touch you stopped me."

"But in your culture—"

"Fuck my culture." His voice was ragged and tired.

The possessive note in his declaration wasn't something she was accustomed to but she found she liked it. A lot. Luminet men were protective of their women but sharing a woman between two men was so normal. The fact that Linc refused to do so, even with his own brother, touched something primal deep inside her.

Tentatively she reached up to run her hands over his chest and around his neck. Like a spring releasing, all the tension in his body disappeared when she touched him.

His mouth sought hers without hesitation and when their tongues collided she could barely remember what they'd been talking about. He kissed her as if she were the only woman alive. The hunger that flowed from him was almost frightening. But it didn't scare her.

It turned her on and got her wetter than any man had ever done. All Linc had to do was look at her and she turned to mush. No one had ever done that to her. She widened her thighs as his kiss deepened. The feel of his erection rubbing against her as his tongue delved into her mouth was darkly erotic.

One of his hands cupped the back of her head and the other gently kneaded her breast. Each time he tweaked her nipple, her vagina ached. As if the two pleasure points were connected.

He pulled back slightly and nibbled on her jaw, up to her ear. Even though he'd shaved that morning, he already had stubble growing back. The gentle brushing against her skin sent shivers rolling over her. "I want to taste you," he murmured.

The words heated her entire body. She'd imagined what it would feel like to have his tongue stroking the folds between her legs, but had been too nervous to ask. Last night had been unexpected but she definitely wanted all he had to offer.

He blazed a trail of heated kisses down her body until he knelt in between her spread thighs. Her abdomen clenched as she watched him.

Linc looked up at her for a brief moment and the raw need on his face took her breath away.

He bent down and the first tentative swipe of his tongue had her fisting the sheet beneath her and arching her back.

That was all the encouragement Linc needed. After the way he'd used her body last night, he wanted to take care of her tonight, to show her how much she meant to him. He might not be able to express himself in words but he could show her with his mouth and hands. He'd waited so long to do this.

Running his hands down her inner thighs, he gently held them open as he licked the length of her pink folds. She let out a little moan that made him ache. Which was why he'd kept his trousers on.

Once he'd made the decision to come to her bedroom he'd known he'd have to stay semi-dressed if he wanted to give her foreplay. If his erection touched her bare skin, it would be over for him.

She tasted sweeter than he'd imagined. Delving his tongue between her soft folds, he savored the feel and flavor of her. Even though they were very similar in appearance and both humanoids, his people had subtle differences from hers. His were taller, generally bigger with thicker bone density, and had an ability to elongate their tongues.

When he slightly extended it inside her, she grabbed his head and writhed against his face. As she threaded her fingers through his hair, he couldn't deny the primal satisfaction that roared through him.

Saroya moved against his face, uncaring how little control she showed. What Linc was doing to her should be illegal. The feel of his tongue delving inside her was enough to make her combust.

Holding on to him, she tried to ground herself, but found it impossible. Linc made her lose herself in a way no one ever had. She wanted to just let go and let him dominate her. And now that she'd experienced all he had to offer, the thought of being with anyone else was impossible. Since coming to Lumineta she'd adapted. Or she thought she had. Now she knew she'd never share Linc with anyone and she loved that he wouldn't share her.

Slowing his strokes, he shifted higher and began circling her clit in a steady, rhythmic pattern. The pressure was light yet perfect. As if he knew exactly the right amount of stimulation she needed.

"Linc," she breathed out his name.

His fingers on her inner thighs tightened and he lightly increased his teasing. When his tongue swirled inside her once again, she lost it. The ecstasy that had been building crested as she went into a freefall.

Her orgasm slammed into her with wild abandon. All her muscles tightened as it ripped through her until she was panting and lying practically boneless against the bed.

Linc looked up at her and a small smile played across his face. "Do you know what you taste like?"

The unexpected question made her blush. Her face heated up but she didn't respond. He didn't seem to expect a response though. He climbed up her body and covered her mouth in a heated claiming.

It seemed so intimate considering what he'd just been doing. Before she had time to dwell on it, his big palms slid down her sides and gripped her hips.

He pulled his head back a fraction. "Turn over," he murmured.

She loved the note of command in his voice. It sent shivers of pleasure racing through her. She'd barely attempted to move before he'd flipped her on her knees. The man had such raw strength, it stunned her.

One of his hands slid down her spine in a slow, sensuous move until he ran it across her behind. She looked over her shoulder at him only to find him staring at her body worshipfully.

Her inner walls clenched at the sight. Part of her wondered if she should feel guilt in embracing Linc like this but it was hard to do so when she'd never loved his brother. What they'd shared had been sweet and easy.

There was nothing sweet or soft about Linc. His dark gaze met hers and the dim light from the hallway bounced off his expression, highlighting his scar. Staring at her now, he looked one hundred percent the warrior.

And he wanted to claim her. The knowledge made her ache even more. She wanted him to fill her completely.

As if he read her mind, he plunged into her in a long, hard thrust. Her head fell forward at the intrusion. Her inner walls expanded around his thick length. She savored the way he filled her.

When he took her this way, he hit her so deeply she knew it wouldn't be long until she came again.

Digging her fingers into the bed, she couldn't hold back the groans that tore from her.

"Do you know how long I've fantasized about this?" His unexpected words rolled over her like a warm caress. His hands tightened on her hips and his thrusts increased.

Each time he slammed into her she cried out. Her vagina was already sensitized from her first orgasm and this only intensified her experience.

"You're mine, Saroya," he growled low in his throat.

Her body certainly agreed.

"Say it," he murmured behind her, his words a command.

When she didn't respond fast enough, he stilled inside her. He palmed her stomach and pulled her upright against him. His muscular chest was rigid against her back. She tried to think straight but he pushed so deep inside her in this position, it was difficult.

"Say you're mine, Saroya." His voice rumbled close to her ear and his hot breath on her neck sent shivers skittering over her skin. She *was* his.

"I'm yours, Linc." It was like her words set off an explosion.

He took her rough and hard as he pummeled into her and she gladly welcomed him. As a sharper, more intense climax curled through her, he shouted out her name. The guttural sound mixed with her own cry of ecstasy.

Linc emptied himself into her and even when she was sure he'd finished, his hips still rocked against hers until finally they collapsed against the bed. He was careful not to put all his weight on her, instead rolling to the side and gently stroking down her back. After she caught her breath, she turned over so that she faced him.

Idly, she traced her finger along the lines of chest.

"I love it when you touch me," he murmured.

She smiled at his words. "The feeling is mutual."

He didn't return her smile. Just stared at her with that intensity that sometimes made her nervous.

"What?" Self-consciously she tucked a few strands of hair behind her ear.

With a tight jaw, he shook his head. She didn't care that he didn't want to talk so she scooted closer and wrapped her arm around his waist. When she did, he mirrored the action and pulled her tight.

He was hard again but he didn't make a move to do anything about it. Just gently stroked his hand down her spine.

"Did you ever think about coming to my bedroom before?" he asked.

The sudden question sucked all the air out of the room.

Her eyes widened, but she slowly nodded. "Sort of. I mean, I fantasized about it, but I never would have done it. I didn't think you even really liked me until recently."

He snorted lightly. "I liked you all right," he murmured before kissing her again, this time softer.

Saroya slid closer into his embrace and all coherent thought fled. All Linc had to do was touch her, and she was a goner.

CHAPTER SIX

Saroya walked out of her bedroom, freshly showered. She'd dried her hair so she slipped on a clean, comfortable green shift. After she'd come home from her classes she'd assumed Linc would be home not long after. She'd tried contacting him at the Samio but he'd been unavailable. *All day.*

As she passed through the living room the transport platform blinked and beeped asking for permission to allow someone access inside their home. When she read her friend Brianna's name on the screen, she pressed accept.

Seconds later her redheaded friend stood in the middle of the transport platform. And she looked pissed. Her dark eyes blazed. "Thanks for letting me come over. Do you have any *villana?*"

Saroya nodded, trying not to smile. "Bad day?"

"You could say that. Aeron had the nerve to show up at my office today. He cornered me in front of everyone and asked me to lunch."

She lifted an eyebrow. That didn't sound so bad. "And?"

"Can I get a glass of *villana* first?" she muttered, suddenly losing all her steam.

While Saroya poured them two glasses, she motioned to the back porch. "Let's talk outside." Unlike her friend she lived on the outskirts of the city and they had land for miles surrounding them.

Brianna sat ramrod straight on one of the padded chairs, looking tense and uncomfortable.

Saroya handed her a glass as she sat next to her. It was clear tonight and instead of just one moon, they could see three of their twelve. "So what happened?"

With the bright illumination, it was easy to see her friend's face redden. "I sort of slept with him."

She definitely hadn't been expecting that. For the past twelve moon cycles Brianna had been adamant about not giving in to the Luminet way of life and especially staying away from Aeron because of her intense attraction to the male. "Sort of?"

"Okay, there was no sort of." She covered her face with her hands for a moment then looked back at her. "I'm so embarrassed. I called the office and canceled all my appointments because lunch was not long enough to…well, you know. That man is a machine."

"So why are you upset? I can't imagine it was bad, was it? That man has been after you for a long time." Since practically the moment they'd landed on Lumineta.

"Well, now he seems to think that I'm going to mate with him and Hauk." She took a long swig of her drink.

"Ah, and you have no intention of doing that?"

Brianna shook her head. "No way. I mean, I know you mated with Linc and Gage but I can't wrap my head around the whole thing."

Saroya swallowed hard. She felt bad that she hadn't told Brianna the truth about her and Linc. Leilani knew so maybe she should tell Brianna too. Technically she'd always been mated to the two of them but until very recently she and Linc hadn't officially consummated things. She didn't know if that mattered within the culture or not and for some reason felt bad telling someone else. "So what did you tell him?"

"It all happened so fast. I was enjoying being with him. Then he started talking about the bonding process and how if I wasn't comfortable with Hauk at first they could work out a system and alternate nights. Like I'm some piece of meat! I can't believe he just assumed I'd mate with them. I was still enjoying my post-coital bliss and he starts making all these ludicrous plans. I told him what I thought of his asshole plan and then I told him never to contact me again."

Saroya looked at her over her glass but stayed silent.

"I've never seen him so angry, but he didn't say a word. He just left and now I feel like shit." Brianna finished her *villana* then held her glass out.

Smiling, Saroya poured her another one. She'd brought the bottle outside because she'd known it was going to be one of those nights. "So you don't want to mate with him and his brother?"

"Today was incredible but I had enough trouble keeping up with Aeron. I don't think I could handle both of them. Besides, I'm not cut out to be..." She trailed off and shook her head. "Forget it. Thanks for letting me come over. I really needed to see you, but enough about me. What's going on with you?"

For the next couple hours they talked and caught up on each other's lives but Saroya couldn't help but wonder where Linc was. And she hated that feeling. Things between them had always been awkward but she'd thought things were changing for the better. He'd always been in the back of her head but now she felt crazy thinking about where he was and why he hadn't contacted her all day.

After Brianna left Saroya couldn't even think about sleeping so she went back to her studio. Painting was the only thing that kept her sane when she got upset. When Linc got home tonight they were definitely going to talk. She wasn't sure what kind of relationship he thought they were going to have, but this wasn't it.

* * *

Linc's sense of dread deepened as he swept through the house for the second time. Saroya wasn't anywhere to be found and she wasn't answering her communicator. There was evidence that she'd had someone over but she wasn't here. He'd checked every room.

Twice.

The induction ceremony at the Samio had run late but he'd come home as soon as he could. She'd probably just gone out for a while. He knew she liked to get together with her human friends. But after a few hours passed and she still hadn't returned home—and he couldn't get a hold of her—

raw fear spiked through him. Saroya wouldn't have left him. Right?

Okay, he had to keep a level head about this. Think and evaluate the situation.

First he called her communicator but she didn't answer. It went straight to her voicemail. Next he called Brianna who told him she'd been over at their place but she'd left hours ago. It had been relatively early when the redhead had left so maybe Saroya really had gone out.

He suddenly realized he didn't know much about what she did when he was traveling. Shit. That humming sensation inside him grew worse but he shoved it back down.

Grabbing his communicator, he headed for the travel platform in the living room. He was probably being paranoid. She'd just gone out somewhere. He told himself to go back home and wait for her, but he simply couldn't just wait around. Not when he felt as if he could crawl out of his skin.

Feeling foolish, he left nonetheless. It wasn't as if they'd never talked over the past twelve moon cycles so every single place she'd mentioned, even once, he stopped at. The last place on his list was a Venesian restaurant near where he knew Brianna and Leilani worked.

She wasn't there either.

Leilani. Why hadn't he thought of her? It was really late, closer to dawn than he'd realized but . . . he didn't care. Pulling out his communicator, he called the dark-haired female.

She answered after four beeps, her voice scratchy. "Hello?"

"I'm sorry to wake you up, but I'm looking for Saroya."

"What . . . who is this?" she rasped out.

Who the hell did she think it was? "Linc," he said through gritted teeth.

"Linc . . . oh, right. How late is it . . . hell, the sun's almost up. Wait, you can't find Saroya?" Now she sounded more awake. "What's going on, have you called the peace keepers? Is she okay?"

"Nothing has happened. I came home late and she wasn't home and hasn't returned." He didn't think this was a case for the peace keepers. Goddess, he hoped not. Crime on Lumineta was so rare, but another surge of panic blasted through him. "Do you know of places she likes to go?" Somewhere he hadn't thought of.

"I dunno, she's normally working so much she falls asleep in her studio. Have you tried that great

Venesian place? I know they stay open twenty-four-seven."

Work. He hadn't even thought of her studio. Feeling suddenly foolish and relieved, he said, "I'll contact you when I find her. Thank you."

After disconnecting, he hurried to the nearest travel platform two blocks away, not caring that he was racing around like a madman. He couldn't believe he hadn't thought of the studio. Now he just hoped she was actually there. If she wasn't, he didn't know what he'd do.

* * *

Bleary eyed, Saroya opened the back door of her home. She'd fallen asleep in her studio again. When Linc was traveling she tended to stay out there more often but when he was home she slept here. Some part of her just felt safer when he was around.

Their house was eerily quiet as she stepped into the kitchen. Surprised Linc hadn't woken her, she started to head for his bedroom when the familiar beep of the transport platform sounded.

He was just getting home *now*? Right before dawn?

Before she'd taken more than a couple steps across the stone floor Linc appeared in the doorway of the kitchen.

He let out a long breath that sounded a lot like relief. "Saroya."

"Are you just getting home?" She knew for a fact that the Samio didn't keep senior instructors overnight. And he looked all disheveled and rumpled. She took a step closer as the scent of perfume filled in the air. Lots of it.

"Yes, I—"

She snatched up the nearest thing she could get her hands on, a ceramic mug, and threw it at his head.

"Hey!" Ducking out of the way, he hurried into the kitchen moving toward her fast.

The mug crashed somewhere in the distance, but she didn't care. She grabbed something else, a glass this time. Hauling her arm back, she never got the chance to throw it before Linc grabbed her wrist, pulling her flush against his body. His grip didn't hurt, but he was immovable.

She yanked her arm back and he immediately let her go. "Saroya, what the devil are you doing?"

She set the glass back on the counter and tried to move away from him, but he had her caged in against the counter. "You've been out all night and smell like an off-world brothel."

"I've been out all night looking for you! I came home and couldn't find you. I finally thought to call Leilani and she said something about you sleeping in your studio. I hadn't even thought to check there." His breathing was ragged, his pupils slightly dilated as he watched her.

She shook her head, not sure she believed him. "I didn't go out to my studio until late."

"We had an induction ceremony and it ran late." He said it so matter-of-fact, and for a brief moment she doubted herself.

But she knew she wasn't overreacting. He'd been keeping himself distant from her even though they'd already crossed an invisible boundary. "Okay, say I believe you. You came home and couldn't find me so you went looking for me. I was here all day and fully available. You couldn't have contacted me so I wouldn't worry anytime yesterday?"

"I'm not used to this whole being mated thing," he finally muttered.

She narrowed her gaze at him. Linc wasn't stupid and from what she knew of him, he wasn't insensitive. "Don't hand me that. What is going on with you? It's like you're purposefully keeping me at arm's length."

He scrubbed a hand over his buzz cut. Finally he met her gaze with his searing dark eyes. "When I came home last I thought you'd left. I couldn't find you anywhere. I thought you'd . . . left me," he repeated in a ragged voice.

Oh, damn. She wanted to reach out and comfort him but held back because she wasn't sure where he was going with his line of thought. "Why did you think that?"

He shrugged, the action jerky. "I don't know. I keep thinking that if I let you into my life you'll be taken from me. Or you'll leave. I'm not like my brother and—"

"I didn't love Gage," she blurted before she could stop herself.

Linc stared at her in surprise. "What?"

Her face heated at the admission, feeling as if she'd shamed Gage's memory, but it was true. "When they rescued us, we didn't understand your culture at first. I thought we'd be forced into mating with *any* two males so I...aligned myself with Gage because he was non-threatening. I knew he'd never hurt me. Only too late I realized we had a choice but by then I'd already agreed to mate with him…and you." She hated admitting that out loud, especially to Linc, but she knew she needed to. "He assured me you would treat me with respect but I was still scared until I met you."

"What about after you met me?" His expression was almost unreadable.

"I was excited but you never touched me." He'd told her that he didn't share but he'd never expanded or explained.

In that moment, Linc's face softened. "I was afraid if I did I'd do something I'd regret. I've never felt territorial until I met you and seeing you two together was difficult. It's why I stayed away from the house, even after Gage died."

His words put a lump in her throat but she worked past it. "I'm not going anywhere, but you have to let me into your life and treat me like a mate, not a roommate." Her voice was low but full of authority.

A shudder snaked through him at her words. When he'd come home tonight and found the house empty, he'd felt his entire world shift. Being able to touch and kiss her the way he'd fantasized about the past few days felt surreal. He'd half convinced himself it was all a dream. It shouldn't please him to learn she hadn't loved Gage but it did on his most primal level. "I don't want you as my roommate, Saroya. I just want you to be mine." He swallowed hard. "And only mine."

Her blue eyes darkened and he knew he'd said the right thing. When she smiled softly, he knew things would be okay between them. It would take time for him to get used to the idea that she wasn't going anywhere, but he'd work past his own bullshit if it meant keeping her in his bed and his life.

They watched each other for a long moment until she finally broke the silence. "I think you need to shower off the scent of all those perfumes. It's making me a little crazy."

He liked that she was feeling territorial of him. His throat thick with emotion, he nodded and stripped off his tunic. He didn't mind showering as long as she came with him. For how he felt now, he didn't want her out of his sight.

The smile disappeared from her face as she bent down and lifted her shift over her head. She wore nothing underneath. The sight of her pink nipples and soft thatch of dark hair between her legs had his entire body tensing. Before he could completely enjoy the soft lines and curves of her body she turned on her heel and headed toward his room.

Watching the way her bare ass swayed made his cock swell to the point of pain. Trailing after her, he followed as she continued toward his bathroom.

The large room was all stone and tile and mirrors. It was cold but with her there, the room was on fire. He felt as if he'd combust any second just staring at her.

She turned the water on with voice command then stepped into the stone enclave. Unlike in her washroom there was no door to pull back. Just a wall of stone and glass blocking off the tiled shower area.

Saroya stepped under the streaming jets and let the water cascade over her lithe body. With her bright gaze on him, she lathered shower gel in her hands and began rubbing it over her arms then chest. He was frozen to the spot as he watched her slow, seductive movements.

Watching her hands moving over her soft breasts and taut, pink nipples made his entire body tense. He wanted to jump her so bad he ached, but held back. Days before when he'd walked in on her touching herself it had been the most erotic thing he'd experienced. Seeing her now felt somehow forbidden even though she was completely aware of his presence.

As she cupped one of her breasts and began slowly teasing her nipple with her thumb his hard length jutted forward. Like a guided missile, it wanted inside her tight sheath.

Quickly he shucked his trousers and let them fall soundlessly to the floor. With even, purposeful movements he stalked toward her.

It was almost imperceptible but Saroya shuddered as he came at her. He loved that he drew that reaction from her. The heat and need he saw in her eyes was so raw and real it floored him. She'd always been so quiet around him before. Not now. Now she let him know exactly what was on her mind. The knowledge relieved him because on her most primal level, she trusted him.

When he neared her, splashes of the hot water ricocheted off her, spraying him, but he was barely aware of the sensation. All he could focus on was Saroya.

She reached for him but he grabbed her wrists and held them above her head as he backed her up against the wall. As her back made contact with the tile she instantly arched it. The motion pushed her breasts out and he couldn't resist bending and taking one in his mouth.

As he ran his tongue over her slick, wet skin she groaned. The sound reverberated around the small enclosure, driving him crazy. Moving against her, his hardness rubbed over her lower abdomen. He wanted to thrust into her but first he wanted to tease her. Enjoy their time together.

She lifted one of her legs and wrapped it around him. The action opened her thighs wider. When her folds rubbed against his hard length he moaned against her nipple.

He let her arms go and Saroya dug her fingers into his shoulders, gripping him hard. "Fuck me, Linc."

Coming from her, the abrupt words made his head snap back. The fire in her eyes was enough to set him off. Without responding he plunged deep into her.

When he did, her mouth parted and almost instantaneously she pushed up and wrapped her other leg around his waist. The action let him sink deeper inside her.

Her inner walls molded around him with a frightening familiarity. Getting used to her, to this, could kill him. But he didn't care. He had to take the chance on them. Hell, she was already under his skin in a way no one else ever would be. The woman had gotten past all his defenses with her quiet grace.

Water sprayed both of them but his body blocked most of it. Not that it mattered. Drops of water dotted her entire lean body and her long, dark hair was slicked back. A few wet locks fell over her chest, framing each breast. The sound of the water rushing around them added to the privacy of this moment. For how he felt, they were the only two people on the planet right now.

She stared at him but her fingers tightened on his shoulders. She'd been wet but still tight. Probably not completely ready for him. Her chest moved up and down as she breathed erratically. Somehow he kept himself still inside her when all he wanted to do was slam into her again and again.

Holding her hips, he kept her firmly against the wall as he bent to take her other nipple between his teeth.

As he flicked his tongue over it, her head fell forward and she pulled his earlobe between her teeth. "You don't have to be so gentle, Linc."

Taking him by surprise, she nipped his neck and scraped her teeth over him. His hips jerked in reaction and in response her inner walls tightened around him. If she kept this up he wouldn't last long.

Saroya didn't want gentle right now. She wanted Linc to lose control. Around her, the man always seemed to have a tight control on himself until they got naked. And she loved that she could make him let go.

He was holding her up with his strength and weight and she wanted to take advantage and explore his body. He'd been abrupt when he thrust inside her but it was exactly what she needed. Having him stretch and fill her got her wetter instantly.

When she ran the pads of her thumbs over his flat brown nipples, he shuddered. The action was slight but she didn't miss it. Using her nails this time, she flicked the tiny buds. They were already hard under her attention and this time his entire body jolted at the contact.

Meeting his gaze, she trembled as his eyes darkened. He was going to give her what she asked for. With his big hands he held her hips tightly. She kept her legs wrapped around him and without warning, he pulled out and slammed back into her.

The motion was abrupt and shaky, as if he were trying to control himself but failing. He didn't make an attempt to kiss her. Just kept his gaze on her while he repeated the action.

When he thrust inside her again she couldn't hold back the cry that escaped. In this position he filled her completely. If he kept slamming into her she knew it wouldn't be long until she came.

Each time he filled her, he hit that perfect spot deep inside her, pushing her closer to climax.

"You're so fucking perfect, Saroya." His voice sounded gravelly and rough. He didn't stop his thrusts as he spoke.

The muscles in his arms flexed as he held her up while still pushing into her.

"So tight," he continued.

"Ah," she cried out as her inner walls began tightening around him. It wouldn't be long now.

"I used to think about you while I used my fist," he muttered, the words barely audible.

As she rolled her hips against his, she cried out again. "Oh God!"

"You're on my mind all the damn time, woman." How he could talk while he was wildly thrusting was beyond her. She could barely remember her own name.

Closing her eyes, she let her head fall back against the tile as an orgasm ripped through her.

The pleasure pulsed from between her legs to all her nerve endings with abandon.

When he reached between them and tweaked her clit, she totally lost it. The intensity of her climax rose inside her until she felt as if she'd fall apart. The sensations surging through her made her body tingle until she was only aware of him.

He was thick and hard and all hers. As she came down from her high she opened her eyes to find him staring at her. His expression was heated but still hard to read.

As he moved them away from the wall he didn't say a word. Instead, he sat on the built-in bench while still buried deep inside her. In that moment she understood what he wanted because she craved it too.

Her knees pressed on the stone bench as her legs settled around his thighs but it didn't hurt. Just the feel of his thick length took away any discomfort. Rising up on her knees, she savored the way he dragged against her inner walls.

When she sat back on him, he hissed out a breath. In this position he was giving her all the control and power. Something that surprised her. She loved that he allowed himself to be vulnerable with her. Would give her this control.

The warm water splashed over her now, creating a waterfall over their bodies. The added sensation was wildly erotic.

She continued slowly moving up and down and savoring the way his body tensed with each stroke. The man was rock-hard and pulsing inside her but she enjoyed dragging this out. Teasing him.

When she slowed her movements even more, Linc lost his patience and took over. His neck muscles corded and his arms tensed. He grabbed her hips and slammed up into her. The hard action sent delicious shivers coursing through her.

She tried to brace her hands on the wall behind him but it was useless. The tile was too slick. As he continued thrusting in jerky, uncontrolled strokes, she could only hold on to him for support. She should have known he wouldn't let her stay in charge for long.

"Saroya," he growled her name, his voice low and intense.

That sound alone made her go weak. Everything about this warrior did. After tonight she knew there would never be anyone else for her. Even the thought was insane.

Almost immediately he began climaxing. His grip on her tightened and his thrusts increased.

With a loud shout he emptied himself inside her. After what felt like an eternity, they both stilled and Linc pressed his forehead against the middle of her chest.

His breath was hot and when he pressed his lips against her skin softly, reverently, she shuddered. He could go from rough and hard to sweet and gentle in seconds. His hands moved from her hips and slid up her back. Gently, he shifted her and pulled her so that she was sitting across his lap.

The way he cradled her against his hard body was dominant and protective at the same time. When he buried his head against her neck, she melted and wrapped her arms around him.

"I started to contact you at least a dozen times earlier yesterday. Then when I got home and you weren't here I really did call. A lot." Linc said quietly.

She stroked her fingers through the damp strands of his hair. "Why didn't you call during the day?"

"I didn't want to seem needy."

She smiled at the blunt, honest answer. "That's not needy. I need to know you care."

He snorted softly. "I care all right. I was half in love with you that first week we met. After that, it was all downhill for me," he murmured.

Surprised, she stiffened slightly and his grip increased as he looked up at her. "I don't expect you to say anything right now, but I need you to know how I feel. I fucked up trying to keep my distance from you and that's something that's going to change. I'll be home so often you'll get sick of me."

Saroya smiled at the last statement. "That's not possible." She felt as if she'd been living in a cold tomb for the past six moon cycles. Now that she and Linc had finally connected everything had changed overnight. If she was honest, she didn't even mind the thought of arguing with him. At least then they were communicating. "You know I—"

He covered her mouth with his hand. "Don't feel you have to say it."

She licked him and when he still didn't move, she used her teeth. When he withdrew his hand she didn't waste time. "I've wanted you from the moment we met. When I found out you had my studio built for me—"

"You knew that was me?"

She nodded. "Yes. And quit interrupting. When I found out what you'd done, you stole a little piece of my heart. After these last few days . . . I love you too, Linc. We still have a lot to learn about each other but I know what I feel."

He grinned and the action completely transformed his face. No longer was he the hard warrior but a man who could make her melt with one smile. When she lightly shivered, Linc used voice command to turn the water off, then scooped her up as he stood. "You need food because tonight is not over. Not by a long shot."

Wordlessly she smiled as he began toweling her off and got distracted. When his hands moved over her breasts, his breath hitched and he paused to cup them. Teasingly, he rubbed his thumb over one of her nipples and let out a small groan. Her smile widened. Looked like food would have to wait.

EPILOGUE

Two moon cycles later

Linc sighed as he stepped off the travel platform, exhausted from training the newest class today. Hell, all week. All he'd been able to focus on was getting home to Saroya. He'd even turned down an off-planet mission. Didn't matter that it would have been only a quarter moon cycle, he didn't want to leave her right now. He knew she could handle it, but things were still too new between them.

The house was quiet, letting him know she was probably still in her studio. Stripping off his belt and tunic, he left them on the island in the kitchen and headed out the back door.

When he entered her studio, his heart rate kicked up about a hundred notches. Saroya was in front of a huge canvas, her back to him, wearing a paint splattered apron—and nothing else. The bow securing it behind her back landed right above her tight ass.

She glanced at him over her shoulder, her expression wicked. "I was hoping you'd be home soon."

"Is that right?" he asked, striding toward her, drinking in every inch of her as she turned to fully face him.

His body simply reacted in her presence. If she was naked, he was hard. Simple as that.

Her lips pulled up, her eyes going heavy-lidded as she watched him move. When she stared at him like that, so unabashed, her need for him so clear, it did crazy things to his heart.

In response, she reached behind her back and pulled the tie on her apron free. Lifting it over her head, she tossed it onto the sheet covered floor. That was when he noticed she'd also stretched out a big canvas on the floor.

"I was thinking we could have naked fun with paints." She ran her hands up his chest and linked her fingers around the back of his neck, pressing her body to his.

When her breasts rubbed against him, he shuddered. "I'm game," he murmured before capturing her mouth with his.

For this woman he would do anything. He'd never imagined finding a woman like her, never thought he'd want to mate with someone more than he wanted his next breath. Now that he'd found her, he was never letting her go.

Thank you for reading Heated Mating. I really hope you enjoyed it. If you'd like to read more turn the page for a peek at some of my other work.

If you don't want to miss any future releases, please feel free to join my newsletter. I only send out a newsletter for new releases or sales news.

Find the signup link on my website: http://www.savannahstuartauthor.com

CLAIMING HER WARRIORS
Copyright © 2013 Savannah Stuart

Brianna hurried into the medical building, thankful that it was only four blocks from where she worked. Her flat sandals made a soft scuffing sound as she crossed the tile floor into the main lobby. Unlike the long-destroyed hospitals from her home planet, Lumineta had what they called medical buildings.

They were five-story dome-shaped buildings with skylights that flooded the structure with natural light. There was only one in each city on the planet because they weren't in use much except for when the warriors were injured. Diseases were almost unheard of except for a few odd cases, as were injuries. And the Luminet people weren't at war with anyone right now. They kept their world well protected.

Before she'd made it to the information desk, a female healer wearing a sage green tunic and matching pants approached her. "Are you here for Aeron?"

Brianna nodded, surprised the healer knew that. "Yes, how—"

"Saroya told me she'd called you and I knew you'd be human like her." The healer smiled gently.

Saroya was Brianna's best friend and one of the few human women rescued over twelve moon cycles ago. Like the other human females now living here, she would have been recognizable by her shorter height alone. But Brianna had red hair, a rarity in this place, so she stood out even more.

She'd met Saroya on the long ride here from their now dead blue planet, and the two of them had been close ever since. Saroya was mated to Linc, another warrior and friends with Aeron a man who...well, a man who meant a great deal to Brianna even if he was frustrating.

The healer pointed to one of the transport platforms. "He's in room 515."

Before she could ask if Aeron was okay, the woman had turned and was walking toward another healer. Well, Saroya would have told Brianna if Aeron had been seriously injured, wouldn't she? Her friend's message had been brief but she hadn't sounded too worried. Brianna's heart rate jumped up a notch as she hurried to the transport platform. She placed her hand on the scanner then typed in the room code. Seconds later she was flashed to Aeron's room.

Blinking as the bright light faded, it took a moment for her to adjust to her surroundings. She'd been living on Lumineta for a while and she still hadn't gotten used to their way of fast travel. It was only possible for short distances, but it was a little disorienting. As her surroundings came together she saw Aeron standing next to a bed large enough to accommodate his six foot seven inch frame. His back was to her and he was pulling his tunic over his head as if he planned to leave.

She stepped from the round, raised platform, hurrying toward him. "What are you doing? You shouldn't be out of bed." Okay, she didn't know that for sure, but he had a big bandage wrapped around his shoulder and under his left arm.

He appeared surprised to see her. His blond hair was rumpled, but those green eyes were piercing and assessing as he raked a hungry gaze over her. It took him a moment to speak. "It's just a training accident, I'm fine," he said gruffly.

Aeron's expression softened as he watched her. Then, it was as if he changed his mind. "But maybe you're right, I am feeling tired." In a few fluid movements, he stripped his tunic back off and laid on the bed. Stretched out on his back like that he looked like a golden god. Like one of the Vikings from her history books. Muscular, toned, taut... Her eyes trailed the length of his long, lean body from chest to toe then she immediately felt guilty.

When she met his gaze he was watching her with barely concealed lust. Like always—ever since they'd met. Burying what that evoked inside her, Brianna hurried to the side of the bed and perched on the mattress.

"Saroya left a message that you were injured, but didn't give me any details. What happened?" Unable to stop herself, her eyes roved over his chest and arms again. Other than the white bandage covering whatever had happened to him, he looked good enough to eat.

"It was just a training exercise. No big deal." His deeply spoken words drew her eyes back up to his face. He watched her intently and all she could think about was their last time together. It had been one moon cycle ago but the way he was looking at her now made her feel like it had happened yesterday.

He'd made her come first with his hands, then his mouth, then... She couldn't even think about that day. As she felt warmth spreading up her neck and cheeks she cursed her fair coloring. Thanks to being a redhead she was cursed with showing all her emotions.

"I'm glad you came to see me though," he murmured, that deep voice rolling over her like liquid sin. "I've missed you." The words seemed to be torn from him, as if admitting that was difficult.

She swallowed hard. "I've missed you too." One moon cycle wasn't that long, but it had sure felt like it. And after receiving that call from Saroya she realized that whatever issues she had with Lumineta's custom of male-female-male joining, she had to get over it if she wanted to be with Aeron. If she had to mate with his brother too, well, they would make it work.

When Brianna heard he'd been injured, her entire world had tilted on its axis. She didn't want to live without Aeron.

He appeared surprised by her words, but he moved lightning fast as he grabbed her hips and pulled her over his lap so that she was straddling his waist. "How much did you miss me?" The wicked tone she recognized was there along with his impressive erection pressing against the juncture of her thighs. Her nipples tightened and her inner walls clenched in anticipation of what she knew he could do to her body. Too bad they had so much clothing in the way.

With the intention of moving off him, she placed her hands on his chest. He'd been injured and she didn't want to make it worse. All that power thrumming under her fingers made her shiver and instead of pushing, she curled her fingers against him. "You're hurt and—"

"And you can make me feel better." She wasn't sure why it happened every time he spoke in that low tone, but it was like his words just wrapped around her, making her entire body tingle in awareness.

"I don't think you're hurt at all," she muttered, but didn't make an attempt to move off him.

CLAIMING HIS MATE
Copyright © 2013 Savannah Stuart

Lauren Hayes shoved a wayward strand of hair under the knit cap she wore as she slid up to the outside back wall of the quiet, two-story house. The black cover over her hair had nothing to do with the chilly October weather. Right now she was all about blending into the shadows this cold fall night. Which meant dressing in all black, like a sneaky burglar.

Because she was about to do something stupid. Incredibly stupid. She inwardly berated herself.

There was no turning back now. Shifters were notorious gossips and word had spread through the grapevine that Grant Kincaid, alpha of the Kincaid wolf pack in Gulf Shores, Alabama was on a honeymoon.

With his new human mate.

That by itself had shocked the shifter world. Kincaid's father had been a brutal bastard—before he'd died. A shitty alpha who'd hated anyone who wasn't supernatural. Or at least that's what Lauren had heard.

The current alpha was two hundred years old and she was twenty-five so it wasn't as if they'd ever run in the same circles. She'd also heard Grant wasn't like his father and from the brief meeting she and her pride had with him six months ago, she had to agree that he seemed pretty decent.

Even if he was a stubborn ass who refused to give her family back what was rightfully theirs. Now that the alpha was out of town, she and some of her pridemates had decided to break into his house.

To steal from him.

Maybe steal was a bit of a stretch, she thought as she moved against the side of the house. Wind whipped around her, sending another shiver racing through her. She was simply taking back something that belonged to her family's pride. She had to remind herself of that. Her sister was getting married in two weeks and the broach the elder Kincaid had taken from her family almost a hundred years ago was supposed to have been a wedding gift when the oldest Hayes daughter got married. The piece of jewelry had been in their family for centuries. Well, the jewels had been. Three, four-carat—*colorless*—diamonds and a handful of emeralds had been passed down from oldest daughter to oldest daughter in some form of jewelry ever since. When Lauren's mother had received a necklace from her mother, she'd had the jewels put into a broach instead.

And Lauren desperately wanted to give it to her sister Stacia as a wedding gift. She deserved it.

Since Lauren was one of the few shifters on the planet who could mask their scent from other shifters, vampires and pretty much all supernatural beings, she'd been more or less volunteered for the job by her cousins. She also had a knack for breaking into places. Not that she was normally a thief. Her cousin Tommy, however, was. When she'd been twelve he'd taught her a lot of tricks, including picking locks and hotwiring cars. Her parents had been so pissed when they'd found out. After she stole back what was rightfully theirs, she bet they'd be glad she had those extra skills. Of course they'd be angry at her for doing this, but she'd known if she told them they would have ordered her not to. She figured it was better to do this then beg forgiveness later.

She had a few pridemates waiting a mile away in case she ran into trouble, but they had to stay out of sight unless she called them.

Right now they were all on Kincaid territory. Didn't matter that it was a touristy beach town right on the Gulf Coast and that humans had no idea a shifter pack had carved out an area to live here. As a jaguar shifter, she knew she shouldn't be here without permission so if she got caught she was so screwed. Wolves weren't known for being forgiving. And stealing from an alpha? She shoved those thoughts out of her head. If she was scared, she couldn't work.

Here goes nothing.

The two story house was raised like most houses on the beach but he also had an upstairs patio that she planned to use to her full advantage. She shimmied up one of the columns with a preternatural speed and hoisted herself up and over the lattice style barrier. Being a cat, she was nimble and quick on her feet, but it still took strength to do this in human form.

Crouching low to the ground, she carefully looked around the large patio at the closed French doors and then back at the beach. The waves sounded softly about a hundred yards away, the calm methodic rhythm doing little to soothe the nerves punching through her. She was about to break into an alpha's home. So, so, so stupid. But it would make her mother and sister happy.

Thankfully the quarter moon was hidden by clouds, further helping her cover. She'd been watching the Kincaid pack's comings and goings for the last week in preparation for tonight. It was midnight so almost every one of them was at one of the many bars or the hotel Kincaid owned. They all worked together as a big family. Their hours were more like vampires' than shifters', but clearly it worked for the pack because they were ridiculously wealthy.

Owning beach front property anywhere could be pricey, but they also owned an entire condominium building next door to Kincaid's personal residence. At least almost everyone was at work. And even though she knew for a fact they had a security system, she'd thrown a giant boulder through the back French doors a couple days ago in preparation.

Lauren had felt like a total jerk doing it, but she'd needed them to replace the doors. Which they'd done this morning. The chances of them having already replaced the security contact that would be standard with the system on the new doors was about five percent. More like zero percent considering she'd been watching the house practically ever since she'd ruined the doors. And when she hadn't been spying, one of her pridemates had.

As she examined the French doors now she realized the lock was also new. And it wasn't the cheap kind either. But, she was very good at getting into places she shouldn't.

Less than sixty seconds later she was inside the master bedroom. After a quick perusal of the top part of the door frame she breathed a sigh of relief to see no new contacts in place. Carefully closing the door behind her, she paused and glanced around the giant room. With her supernatural eyesight she didn't need to turn on a light to see everything—not that she would anyway. Might as well just put up a bright neon sign that she'd broken in.

The furniture was masculine, but there were definitely feminine touches. Not that Lauren cared about any of the décor. Now she was focused on looking for a safe. If he were going to hide diamonds and emeralds, it would definitely be in a safe. There was a slim chance he'd put it in a bank vault, but shifters and vamps, especially one as old as him, were weird about that stuff. No, they liked to keep their valuables close on hand.

For all she knew a silent alarm had gone off. There weren't any visible sensors in the bedroom, but that didn't mean shit. She knew that by breaking in blind without knowing the complete layout of the security system she was taking a chance but almost no one had sensors in their bedrooms. It didn't make sense. Living room areas and downstairs areas of course, but bedrooms and any upstairs saw too much foot traffic on a daily basis.

Moving quickly and quietly she went to the most obvious place to hide a safe. The closet. Nothing there. She searched behind picture frames next, then everywhere else she could think of before moving to the next room. The door was open to reveal an office.

Pausing, she could hear only the wind and waves outside. There were residual scents in the house but that made sense. She stepped inside the room, her boots silent against the rich hardwood floor. Two steps in, she realized she wasn't alone. It was like an abrupt assault on her senses and her inner animal simply knew.

Before she could turn fully around, she was tackled to the ground by a huge male. Definitely supernatural.

Strong, muscular arms encircled her from behind, throwing her to the ground, the male on top of her. Somehow he managed to angle their fall so he took the brunt of the impact on his arms. All the air left her lungs in a whoosh as panic slammed through her. She hadn't heard him, hadn't even scented him. That alone told her how dangerous he was.

Though all her animal instinct told her to fight, she knew she was at a disadvantage. Going limp, she didn't struggle. The second she was set free or her captor loosened his grip, she was running. Wolves might be strong, but jaguars were wicked fast. In human and shifter form.

"What the hell are you doing sneaking around in wolf territory in *my* alpha's fucking house?" a familiar male voice said near her ear, a trickle of his fresh scent that reminded her of the beach in winter enveloping her.

She hadn't scented him before, probably because of her own fear and panic at doing such a stupid thing—but now his scent covered her. She shivered at the sound of Max McCray's voice. Kincaid's second-in-command. He was supposed to be at the Crescent Moon Bar tonight working.

Lauren swallowed hard. "I want *my* family's fucking jewels back," she gritted out. There was no sense in lying. He'd be able to scent the bitter, acidic stench if she tried. She could normally cover her scent well, but right now she was nervous and couldn't keep her gift under control. Blind panic hummed through her, her inner jaguar telling her to run, run, *run*.

But she couldn't. Not with Max's massive body on top of her, keeping her pinned in place.

She was ashamed to admit that she'd had more than a handful of fantasies about the dark-haired, muscular shifter with the piercing blue eyes. None like this, with her flat on her stomach and him behind her... Okay, that was a lie. She'd had those types of fantasies too. Of course they'd both been naked and she hadn't been working as a thief.

COMPLETE BOOKLIST

Miami Scorcher Series
Unleashed Temptation
Worth the Risk
Power Unleashed
Dangerous Craving
Desire Unleashed

Crescent Moon Series
Taming the Alpha
Claiming His Mate
Tempting His Mate
Saving His Mate

Futuristic Romance
Heated Mating
Claiming Her Warriors

Contemporary Erotic Romance
Adrianna's Cowboy
Tempting Alibi
Tempting Target
Tempting Trouble

ABOUT THE AUTHOR

Savannah Stuart is the pseudonym of *New York Times* and *USA Today* bestselling author Katie Reus. Under this name she writes slightly hotter romance than her mainstream books. Her stories still have a touch of intrigue, suspense, or the paranormal and the one thing she always includes is a happy ending. She lives in the South with her very own real life hero. In addition to writing (and reading of course!) she loves traveling with her husband.

For more information about Savannah's books please visit her website at: www.savannahstuartauthor.com.

Printed in Great Britain
by Amazon.co.uk, Ltd.,
Marston Gate.